TREE SPIRITS

The Story of a Boy Who Loved Trees

Story and Illustrations by

Florence Baker Karpin

The Countryman Press
Woodstock, Vermont

Library of Congress Cataloging-in-Publication Data
Karpin, Florence B.
    Tree spirits / story and illustrations by Florence Baker Karpin.
    Summary: A small boy who loves trees comes under the spell of a tree spirit whose message
  "the forests are the lungs of the earth" inspires him to dedicate his life to reforesting the world.
  ISBN 0-88150-248-0: $14.00
  [1. Trees–Fiction. 2. Conservation of natural resources–Fiction.] I. Title.
  PZ7.K1484Tr 1992
  [E]—dc20   92–19377
                                                                                                          CIP
                                                                                                                    AC

10   9   8   7   6   5   4   3   2   1

Published by The Countryman Press, Inc., P.O. Box 175,
Woodstock, Vermont 05091

Art direction: Rachel Kahn
Typesetting: Barbara Homeyer, Lebanon, NH

For Gary, Emily, and Priscilla

There was once a boy who loved trees more than anything else. He loved them not as most boys do—for sturdy branches to climb, and smooth, broad trunks to carve with names.

He loved the trees just for themselves.

Every day when school was done, the boy would go deep into the woods which fringed his grandmother's garden, and he would not come home till the sun had sunk behind the dusky hills.

"Why do you always go into the forest, Jacob?" asked his grandmother as she sat by the stove darning his woolen stockings. "What is in the woods but the deer and rabbits who hide from you?"

The boy looked up from his book. "The trees are why I like to go, Nana," he told her. Then after a thoughtful moment he added, "The trees are my friends, you know. Sometimes they speak to me."

His grandmother smiled knowingly. "Your papa, when he was alive and well, knew the forest too."

"I am just like my papa," laughed the boy. Then his grandmother gathered him onto her lap, and together they rocked by the warmth of the stove till bedtime.

There was a tree growing in the forest, in a small grassy clearing, which Jacob loved more than any other. The elm stood tall and grand, its lofty crown arching high against the sky. It seemed to the boy to reach the very dome of heaven.

Whether the day dawned gray or fair, Jacob would go to the woodland elm. When the summer's rain pattered upon its leaves, he would clasp the tree's broad trunk and listen to the leaves' song. And in winter, when all the wood stood deep in snow, the boy would trudge through the drifts to hear the elm's empty branches whisper to the wind.

Perhaps it was because he so loved the trees that Jacob came to know their secrets. The trees knew where the birds go in the winter, and where the storms are born. They knew where the red fox runs and what the owl speaks of, in the moonlight. And the boy heard and understood all that they told him.

O ne autumn day when the trees were ablaze with color, Jacob hurried home from school, eager to surprise his grandmother with the bright leaves he had gathered. He paused at the gate. From the forest came the sound of an axe! With each thudding blow he heard the stricken tree cry out, before it went crashing to the ground.

Jacob bounded toward the woods. When he reached the woodsman, he stopped short. On every side lay fallen trees, their bright foliage already wilting in the sun. The woodsman's axe gleamed as he raised it for another blow. Jacob ran to him and clung to the man's arm. "Oh please, Sir! Don't cut down the trees!" he pleaded. "They are living beings, too!"

"Be off with you!" growled the woodcutter, shoving the boy aside. "Would you keep an honest man from gathering his fuel, with winter near upon us?"

Jacob fought against his tears. "But, couldn't you take just the dead trees?"

"I'll take what I want, with no advice from the likes of you!" retorted the man. Then, as he lifted his axe once more, the burly woodsman saw the anguished look on the boy's face. He lowered his axe and looked around at the fallen trees. "Well now," he said, stroking his whiskers, "'Tis likely I've wood enough here to keep me for a season. . . . Yah, I'll call it a day." And taking hold of his horse's bridle, he led his wagonload of logs out of the forest.

Jacob watched him go. With a heavy heart, he listened to the restless trees sighing for their lost companions.

Then the boy became aware of another voice somewhere in the forest, calling to him. The voice was soft and whispery, like those of the trees. He followed the sound, and soon found himself in the clearing where stood the great elm tree.

Within the trunk of the elm hovered a figure! The shining elfin-creature, glimmering in every shade of green, smiled down at him. "Do not be afraid," she said. "I am your friend, the elm tree spirit." She reached for his hand. "Come, I must take you on a journey."

The tree spirit drew the boy up to the top of the elm tree as if he were a feather adrift on the air. Together, they soared above the towering fir trees, over the crowns of the oak and maple, the birch and hickory. Soon the forest stretched far below.

Jacob looked back and watched his grandmother's cottage grow smaller and smaller until it disappeared altogether. The cold rushing wind pressed against his ears and watered his eyes. "Where are we going?" he gasped between gulps of air.

The spirit's voice was close beside him. "We will follow the day across the land of tomorrow," she told him. "You will see what is to happen to the forests."

And so, they sailed westward, the boy and the tree spirit. They sailed into the future, passing over sprawling cities and endless highways where nothing but concrete and asphalt covered the land. They looked down on floods and mudslides where whole mountains had been stripped of timber. They saw rain forests being burned and laid bare.

"The forests are the lungs of the earth," said the tree spirit. "When the forests are gone, so then will all life be gone." As she spoke, the spirit faded to a tiny glimmer, and vanished the moment the boy felt his feet touch the ground.

The elm tree spirit had returned him to her place in the wood. But the tree was no longer adorned with golden leaves. It stood barren, its boughs broken and fallen. The spirit of the elm had departed.

Jacob leaned against the dead tree and gave in to his sorrow. Then lifting his voice for all to hear, he called out: "Tree spirits, hear my vow! I, Jacob, will one day cover the world with your seeds!"

The promise rang through the silent forest.

Every year thereafter, Jacob gathered beechnuts and chestnuts, hazelnuts and acorns from the autumn woodlands, and planted them at the edge of his grandmother's garden. When the tiny tree sprouts appeared in the spring, he tended them until they were hardy seedlings. He then placed them around sunny meadows and along the dusty roads of the village beyond his grandmother's cottage.

One day, when Jacob had become a young man, he said to his grandmother, "The saplings are thriving, Nana. It is time that I begin my mission."

"I know, Jacob," nodded the old woman. "When you were still a boy you told me what you must do. 'Tis time you kept your promise."

Then Jacob said goodbye to his grandmother. With a trowel
in his pocket and a weighty sack of nuts and acorns upon his
back, he set out to keep his vow to the tree spirits.

He walked the land, and wherever he came upon open, windswept places, Jacob planted trees. He traveled far—over mountains, over plains, across rivers, across oceans.

Year after year he walked, on and on through rain and sun and wind, until he had walked the whole broad earth around!

The long hard years bowed him down and weathered him brown as wood bark. There came a day when he was no longer able to plant the trees. Wearily, the old man put away his trowel and turned homeward.

The village he had known as a boy had become a large and bustling town. The people living there would never know who had planted the great spreading trees shading their streets and houses. But Jacob knew, and his heart was glad.

His grandmother's cottage was long gone, yet the forest still stood deep and somber. Jacob looked up to the branches far above him, to the bright flecks of sunlight winking through the leaves.

"Tree spirits!" he called, "I am Jacob, the boy come home!"

His thin, tremulous voice could not carry far, and he called out again, "I kept my promise . . . I sowed the whole earth with your seeds!"

Gradually, there came a low murmuring through the forest. The sound of the trees grew louder. Jacob heard their voices all mingling together, welcoming him home.

Then slowly, his stiffened fingers began to tingle with energy, and his weary arms felt strong. The old man looked down to see tiny green leaves sprouting all along his arms and hands! His bended back straightened, and he felt himself growing sturdy and tall . . . and taller still! At last, he towered amid the topmost branches of the trees!

Joyously, Jacob spread his leafy arms skyward, and there above the clouds, beheld the dome of heaven.